Happy Birthday Tannis!
♡ Jesse +Susan

Kay Fraser—
hero among moms, champion of kids—
this mess is for you!

RATand ROACH
Friends to The End

by
David
Covell

VIKING
An Imprint of Penguin Group (USA) Inc.

This is Rat and his best friend, Roach.
They live here under Avenue A.

" Rat, please don't cross that gutter.
I just cleaned this page."

Ever since the day they met,
Rat and Roach have been side by side,
even when it rains.

They get along great . . .

. . . most of the time.

But sometimes THEY YELL!

"Toothpick, Crabby Head, FLEA!"

"Hair Ball, Tuna Breath, MOUSE!"

And why do they yell?
Why do they shout? Is it because . . .

Rat lets out stink bombs . . .

and Roach sprays too much sweetness?

Or because Rat makes a mess
and Roach makes things too pretty ?

Or Rat has bad manners
when Roach cooks too fancy?

Or Rat hugs
TOO TIGHT !

"ak!"

Or do they yell because . . .

But it's REALLY bad when . . .

Rat BANGS **TOO LOUD** !
whenever Roach tries to sing in the band.

Is this **THE END**?
Will they still be friends?

They woke up and brushed
without saying, "Good morning."

They went to work. But didn't work hard.
Rat thought about Roach . . .

and Roach thought about Rat.

They thought about days when
they used to have fun.

What will make Roach smile ? thought Rat.

What would Rat really, really love ?
wondered Roach.

"Okay Roach! You can sing in the band."

"Really? I made your favorite.
It's Tuna Surprise!"

"Ta-Daaah!"

"You're my best friend, Rat."
"You're my best friend, Roach."

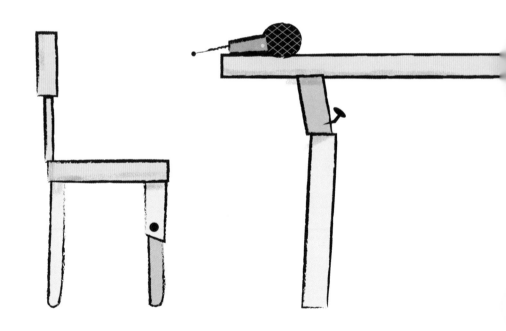

The End.

" Ummm, Rat.
You can let go now."

VIKING ✳ Published by Penguin Group ✳ Penguin Young Readers Group, 345 Hudson Street, New York,
New York 10014, U.S.A. ✳ Penguin Group (Canada), 90 Eglinton Avenue East, Suite 700, Toronto, Ontario, Canada
M4P 2Y3 (a division of Pearson Penguin Canada Inc.) ✳ Penguin Books Ltd, Registered Offices: 80 Strand, London
WC2R 0RL, England ✳ First published in 2012 by Viking, a division of Penguin Young Readers Group
10 9 8 7 6 5 4 3 2 1

LIBRARY OF CONGRESS CATALOGING-IN-PUBLICATION DATA
Covell, David.   Rat and Roach friends to the end / by David Covell.   p. cm.   ISBN 978-0-670-01409-5 (hardcover)
[1. Best friends—Fiction. 2. Friendship—Fiction. 3. Rats—Fiction. 4. Cockroaches—Fiction.] I. Title.   PZ7.C83392Rat 2012
[Fic]—dc23   2011028924 ✳ Manufactured in China ✳ Set in Tempo Medium Grunged

ALWAYS LEARNING   PEARSON

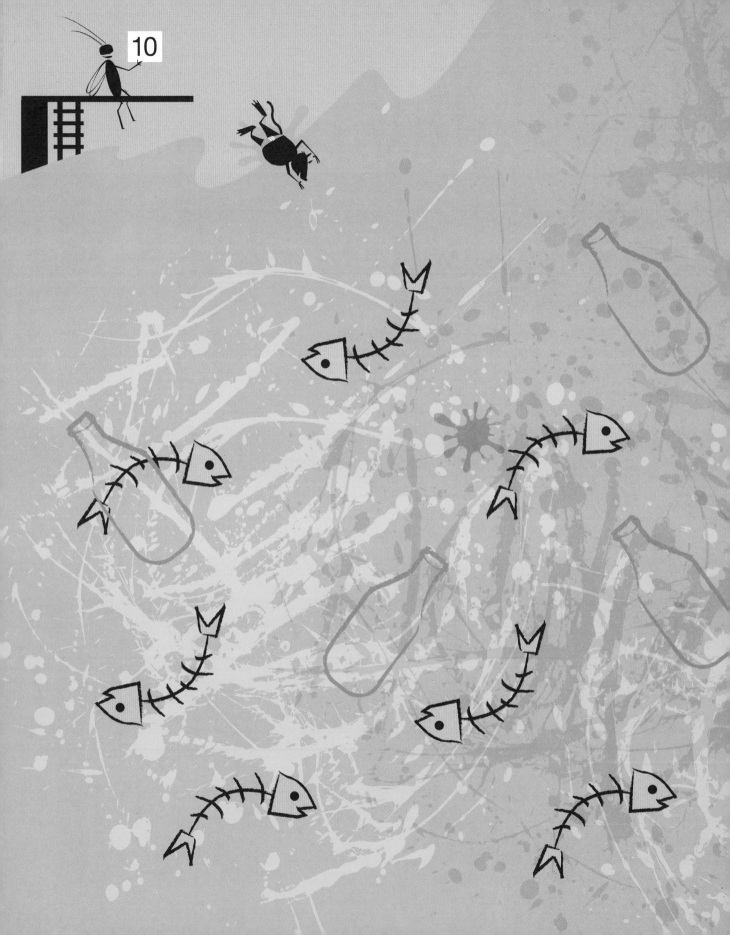